Things My Father Taught Me Through Sports...

PLAYING THE GAME OF

Baseball

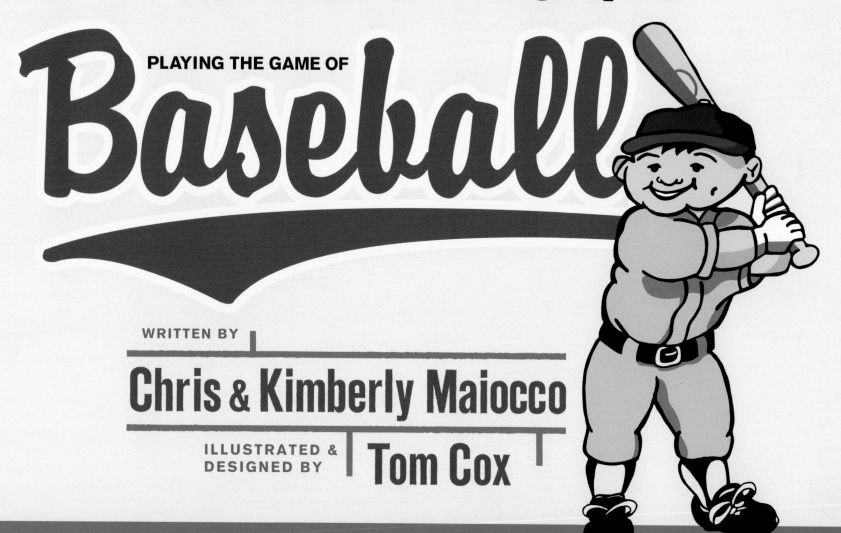

WRITTEN BY

Chris & Kimberly Maiocco

ILLUSTRATED &
DESIGNED BY **Tom Cox**

HIS KIDS
PUBLISHING, INC.
www.hiskidspublishing.com

HIS KIDS
PUBLISHING, INC.
www.hiskidspublishing.com

Text Copyright ©2002 by Chris & Kimberly Maiocco
Illustration and Design Copyright ©2002 by Tom Cox
Edited by Julie Land
Foreword interview by Barb Cash, Unlimited Potential, Inc., www.upi.org
All rights reserved.
Published in the United States of America by His Kids Publishing, Inc.,
P.O. Box 72172, Marietta, GA 30007
Printed in China.

JOHN SMOLTZ

1996 NL CY YOUNG WINNER

4-TIME NL ALL-STAR

MEMBER OF THE 1995 WORLD CHAMPION ATLANTA BRAVES

HOLDS CAREER RECORDS FOR THE MOST POST-SEASON WINS WITH 11

HOLDS NL RECORD FOR MOST SAVES IN A SEASON

ONE OF THE MOST DOMINANT PITCHERS IN MLB OVER THE LAST DECADE

"Dear Lord, I know I have many things in my past for which I need Your forgiveness and Your cleansing and I lay them at Your feet right now. I thank You that You experienced death so that I might experience life and I put my faith and trust in You. I surrender all that I am to You and desire to follow You for the rest of my days. This is my Decision! Amen."

I started my professional baseball career with my hometown team, the Detroit Tigers, in 1984 and was then traded to the Atlanta Braves in 1987. By 1988 I had arrived in the big leagues and began to see my baseball career make an upward swing. In 1991 we went from "worst to first", and found ourselves in the World Series. The first half of that year I was 2-11, but the second half I finished up 12-2 and pitched two of the most important games of my life in the playoffs. The first was the 7th game of the NLCS against the Pirates that put us into the World Series and the second was the 7th game of the World Series. I pitched against Jack Morris for eight-plus innings of shutout ball before I was taken out. We ultimately lost in the 11th inning and I received a no-decision.

Unfortunately, this was fast becoming the theme of my life - "No-Decision". I had attended Baseball Chapel and read the Word of GOD some. I had prayed "the sinner's prayer" many times between 1991 and 1995, thinking I was becoming a Christian. Therefore, I thought I was doing okay. My actions, though, still pointed to a no-decision. I was consumed with what people thought of me and I received my significance from baseball and not a relationship with Christ. In fact, my prayers had been a religious ritual that were not from the heart. I was not saved.

I finally asked myself this vital question that would change my life forever, "If I know what it takes to have a close, personal walk with Christ, then what prevents me from doing it?" The answer I gave changed what and who I am for all eternity. I committed my life to JESUS and quit trying to do things my own way. John 15:5 says, "I am the vine, you are the branches. If a man remains in Me as I am in Him, he will bear much fruit. Apart from Me he will bear nothing." For the longest time I was trying to bear fruit apart from Him, even though I thought I was walking close to Him. Now, because of the personal relationship I have with Christ, I have seen this verse come alive in my life and know that my life is bearing fruit.

In the game of baseball, a pitcher separated from the catcher can do nothing. Their relationship is of the utmost importance for the team. In the game of life, our relationship with our Maker through Jesus is similar, apart from Him we can do nothing. This relationship is of the utmost importance for us to live the 'victory' God desires for us and fulfill our place in the Body of Christ. Trusting in Jesus by faith and turning from sin is essential and a life without applying His Word is a life of "No-Decision".

Are you walking down that road of "No-Decision"? Are you seeking the approval and the applause of men, rather than the Lord? What's keeping you from surrendering your life to the Lord? A life apart from a growing relationship with Christ is a very empty life, but you don't have to settle for that. First you must confess your sins to the Lord and allow Him to cleanse you of them. Then you need to put your trust in Jesus and surrender everything you have and everything you are to Him. It's a very simple process that will profoundly change the course of your life and give you that security we all desire.

John Smoltz

JOHN SMOLTZ

BOOK   **CHAPTER**   **VERSE**

"I am the vine, you are the branches. If a man remains in Me as I am in Him, he will bear much fruit. Apart from Me he will bear nothing."

JOHN 15:5

Hi! My name is Michael. Last year I trusted Jesus as my Savior by faith. Do you know that I love to play baseball? When I grow up I want to play in the big leagues.

MY DAD HAS ALWAYS TOLD ME THAT WHATEVER I DO, **DO IT FOR THE LORD.**

BOOK

COLOSSIANS

CHAPTER

3

VERSE

17

"Let every detail in your lives - words, actions, whatever - be done in the name of the Master, thanking God the Father every step of the way."

THE MESSAGE

Every day I get dressed in my favorite baseball clothes. Do you know what's special about today?

DID YOU KNOW

THAT GOD TELLS US TO GET DRESSED EACH DAY IN HIS ARMOR?

"... Put the belt of truth around your waist. Put the armor of godliness on your chest. Wear on your feet what will prepare you to tell the good news of peace. Also, pick up the shield of faith. With it you can put out all of the flaming arrows of the evil one. Put on the helmet of salvation. And take the sword of the Holy Spirit. The sword is God's word."

BOOK	CHAPTER	VERSE
EPHESIANS	6	14-17

NIrV

Today we are playing the best team in the whole world. We've been practicing really hard for this game. And you know, the more we practice the better we get.

AS A CHRISTIAN, WE NEED TO PRACTICE OUR FAITH SO THAT WE ARE **ALWAYS READY** IN SEASON AND OUT OF SEASON.

BOOK	CHAPTER	VERSE
2nd TIMOTHY	**4**	2

"Preach the word; be ready in season and out of season; correct, rebuke, encourage, with great patience and instruction."

Well, it's time to go to the field. But before I go, I can't forget my equipment - bat, glove, helmet, and water bottle.

Holy Bible

I HAVE LEARNED THAT AS A CHRISTIAN, MY EQUIPMENT IS MY BIBLE.

"All scripture is given by the inspiration of God and is profitable for doctrine, for reproof, for correction, for instruction in righteousness..."

BOOK

CHAPTER

VERSE

2nd TIMOTHY

3

16-17

It's game time and James is our umpire. He likes to watch me play. I really like it when he gives me a high five. He's a Christian; he told me so.

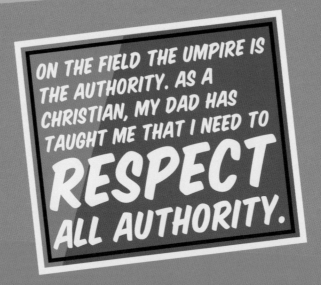

ON THE FIELD THE UMPIRE IS THE AUTHORITY. AS A CHRISTIAN, MY DAD HAS TAUGHT ME THAT I NEED TO **RESPECT** ALL AUTHORITY.

BOOK	CHAPTER	VERSE	
1st PETER	**2**	**13** NIrV	"...submit yourself to every ordinance of man."

Today we are playing an awesome team. They are first in the league. Some of my best friends have come to watch.
Can you see them?

I HAVE BEEN TAUGHT THAT NO MATTER HOW YOUNG WE ARE, AS A NEW CREATION IN CHRIST, WE REPRESENT JESUS. WE MAY BE THE ONLY "BIBLE" SOME PEOPLE WILL EVER SEE.

"Let no one look down on your youthfulness, but rather in speech, conduct, love, faith and purity, show yourself an example of those who believe."

BOOK
CHAPTER
VERSE

1st TIMOTHY

4

12

Before our games we pray. Then our coach, my Dad, tells us where to play. I like to play shortstop and first base, but someday I want to be a pitcher.

MY DAD HAS ALWAYS TOLD ME THAT I NEED TO LISTEN TO MY COACH AND PLAY MY POSITION AS PART OF THE TEAM. AS A CHRISTIAN, GOD IS OUR COACH AND ALL OF US HAVE A POSITION TO PLAY.

BOOK

1st CORINTHIANS

CHAPTER

12

VERSE

18

"But now God has placed the members, each one of them, in the body, just as He desired."

It's the first inning and I am playing shortstop. There is a runner on first with one out. I am in the ready position watching the batter, when SMACK - here comes a pop fly right to me...

THERE ARE BASICS TO EVERY SPORT. IN BASEBALL, THE FOUNDATION TO CATCH A POP FLY IS TO "GET UNDER IT AND USE TWO HANDS."

IN LIFE

CHRIST IS OUR FOUNDATION.

"He is like a man building a house, who dug deep and laid a foundation upon the rock... it had been well built."

BOOK LUKE CHAPTER 6 VERSE 48

I caught it! WOW! The runner forgot to tag up. I need to throw to first. I reach back and throw it hard... GOT HIM! DOUBLE PLAY!

IN THROWING **A BALL,** IT'S VERY IMPORTANT TO BE ACCURATE SO YOU CAN **HIT YOUR TARGET.** AS A CHRISTIAN, WE ARE TO ACCURATELY DELIVER **GOD'S WORD!**

BOOK

2nd TIMOTHY

CHAPTER

2

VERSE

15

"Be diligent to present yourself approved to God as a workman who does not need to be ashamed, handling accurately the word of truth."

Now it's time for my favorite part, batting. I like to try and hit home runs but my Dad tells me to focus on the ball. As I get into the batter's box, I get my bat back, set my feet, and look for the ball. Here comes the pitch...

WHEN BATTING, WE SHOULD KEEP OUR EYES ON THE BALL. AS A CHRISTIAN, OUR EYES SHOULD BE ON **JESUS.**

"I will lift up my eyes to the hills, from whence comes my help? My help comes from the Lord…"

BOOK

PSALM

CHAPTER

121

VERSE

1-2

SMACK! Oh, it is a high fly... don't look, just run. I was almost to first base when I heard the umpire yell, "HE'S OUT!" I flied out to center field. Everyone knew I was sad.

MY DAD

HAS TAUGHT ME THAT I WILL NOT GET A HIT EVERY TIME I AM UP TO BAT. BUT WHAT'S IMPORTANT IS MY ATTITUDE. AS A CHRISTIAN, WE SHOULD HAVE AN ATTITUDE OF JOY.

BOOK

CHAPTER

PSALM

35

VERSE

9

"And my soul shall be joyful in the Lord..."

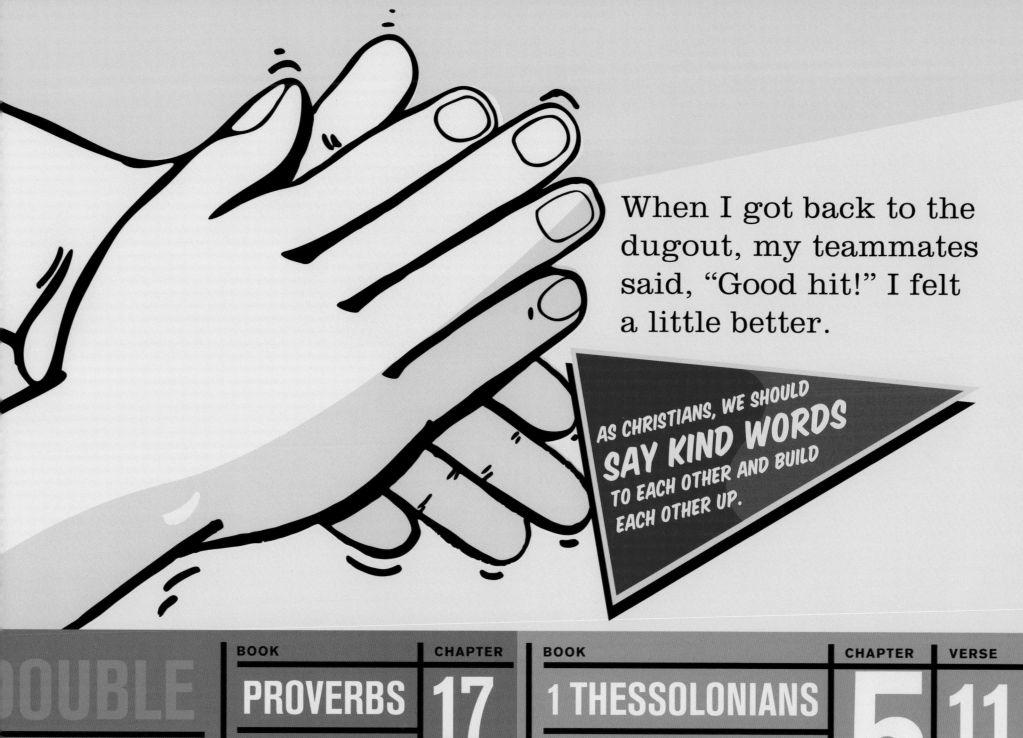

When I got back to the dugout, my teammates said, "Good hit!" I felt a little better.

AS CHRISTIANS, WE SHOULD **SAY KIND WORDS** TO EACH OTHER AND BUILD EACH OTHER UP.

BOOK		CHAPTER		BOOK		CHAPTER	VERSE
PROVERBS		**17**		**1 THESSOLONIANS**		**5**	**11**
		VERSE					
"A friend loves at all times."		**17**		"Therefore, encourage one another, and build up one another, just as you also are doing."			

Well the inning is over and we are on the field again. I was still thinking about my last at bat when I heard the coach say, "Get ready!" A grounder was coming right to me...

The ball went right through my legs. I can't believe I missed it! I let my team down. Now I really feel sad. But my teammates were saying, "Good try Michael; you'll get the next one!"

I HAVE LEARNED FROM MY DAD TO ALWAYS BE READY WHEN ON THE FIELD. DO YOU KNOW WHAT THE BIBLE SAYS ABOUT BEING READY?

IN BASEBALL SOMETIMES YOU MAKE MISTAKES. MY DAD HAS TAUGHT ME THAT AS A CHRISTIAN, EVEN WHEN TIMES ARE TOUGH, JESUS IS WITH ME!

BOOK
1 PETER
CHAPTER
3
VERSE
15
"...always be ready to give a defense to everyone who asks you for a reason for the hope that is in you..."

"... though I walk through the valley of the shadow of death I will fear no evil for you are with me."
BOOK
PSALM
CHAPTER
23
VERSE
4

We are now in the last inning and even with the errors, it has been a good game. The score is tied 3 to 3. The go ahead runner is at third, and I am up to bat. I was dreaming about hitting a home run when Dad stopped me on the way to the plate. "A base hit is all we need to win", he said. I knew he was right and quickly prayed, *Dear Jesus, forgive me for thinking of myself and help me to do what is right for the team!*

DO YOU KNOW THAT JESUS LAID DOWN HIS LIFE FOR US? I HAVE BEEN TAUGHT THAT SOMETIMES I'LL HAVE TO DO WHAT IS BEST FOR OTHERS.

"But He gives a greater grace. Therefore it says, 'God is opposed to the proud, but gives grace to the humble'."

BOOK

CHAPTER

VERSE

JAMES 4 6

I did my best and hit a ground ball right up the middle. The runner scored from third. We won the game! We really won the game! WOW, THIS IS AWESOME!

AS A CHRISTIAN, I HAVE LEARNED THAT WE ARE TO TRY OUR **BEST** IN ALL THINGS.

BOOK
PHILLIPIANS

CHAPTER VERSE
3 | 14

"I press on toward the goal for the prize of the upward call of God in Christ Jesus."

After the game, my friend Logan got the game ball for his great play at third and his terrific attitude. My Dad was proud of us for not losing hope and for playing as a team.

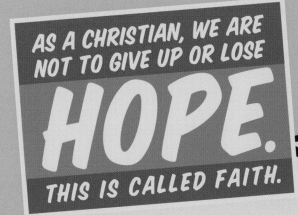

AS A CHRISTIAN, WE ARE NOT TO GIVE UP OR LOSE **HOPE.** THIS IS CALLED FAITH.

"Now faith is the assurance of things hoped for, the conviction of things not seen."

BOOK
HEBREWS
CHAPTER | VERSE
4 | 12

As a treat, we're going to lunch with the team. On the way, Dad told me even though I may win or lose baseball games, I'm a winner in the biggest game of all, life - because I have trusted Jesus as my Savior.

HE'S A GREAT **DAD,** GOD'S A GREAT **GOD,** AND I'M READY FOR THE NEXT GAME.

BOOK

CHAPTER

VERSE

2nd TIMOTHY

4

7

"I have fought the good fight, I have finished the course, I have kept the faith."

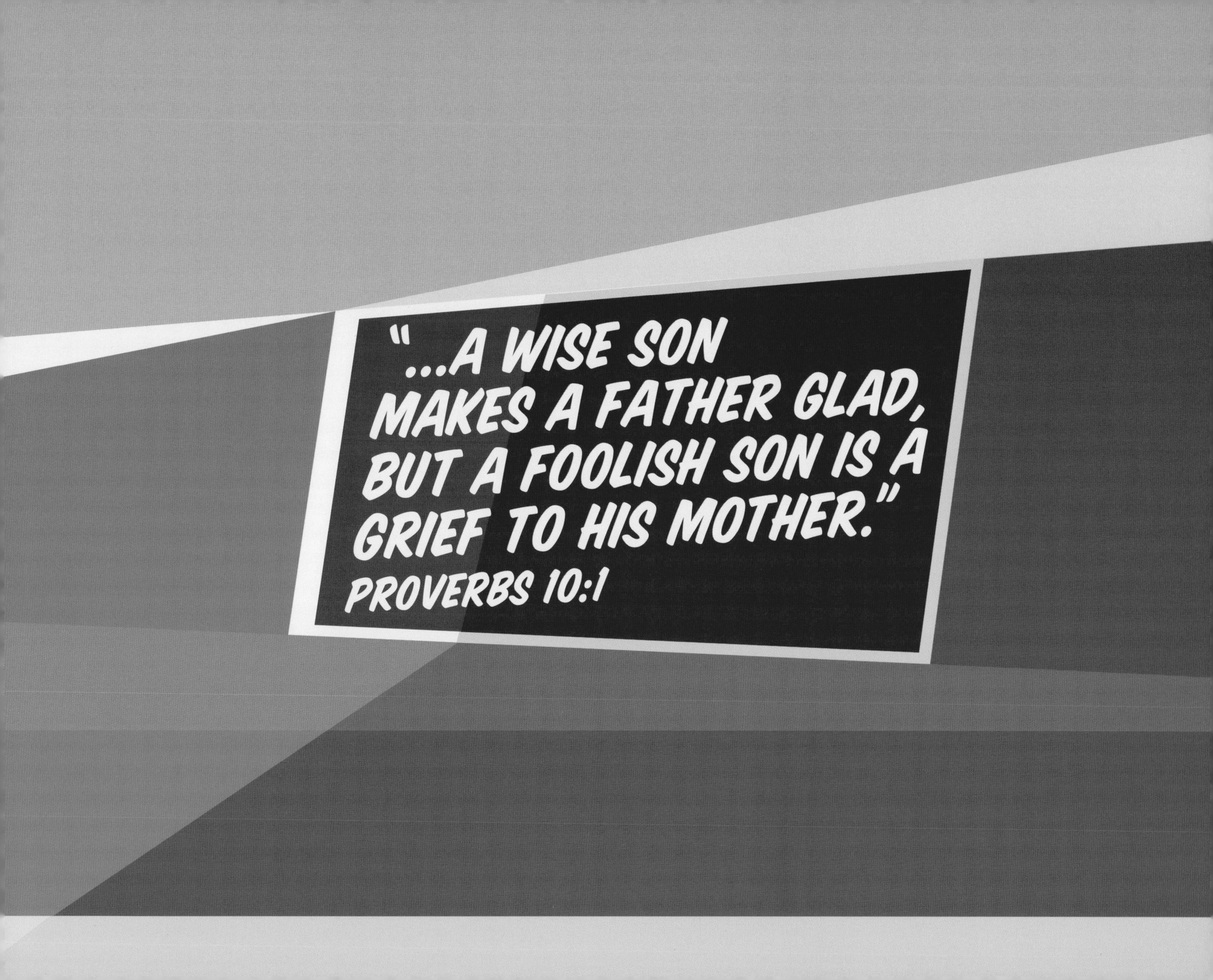
"...A WISE SON
MAKES A FATHER GLAD,
BUT A FOOLISH SON IS A
GRIEF TO HIS MOTHER."
PROVERBS 10:1

HIT A "HOME RUN" IN LIFE BY TRUSTING JESUS AS YOUR SAVIOR!

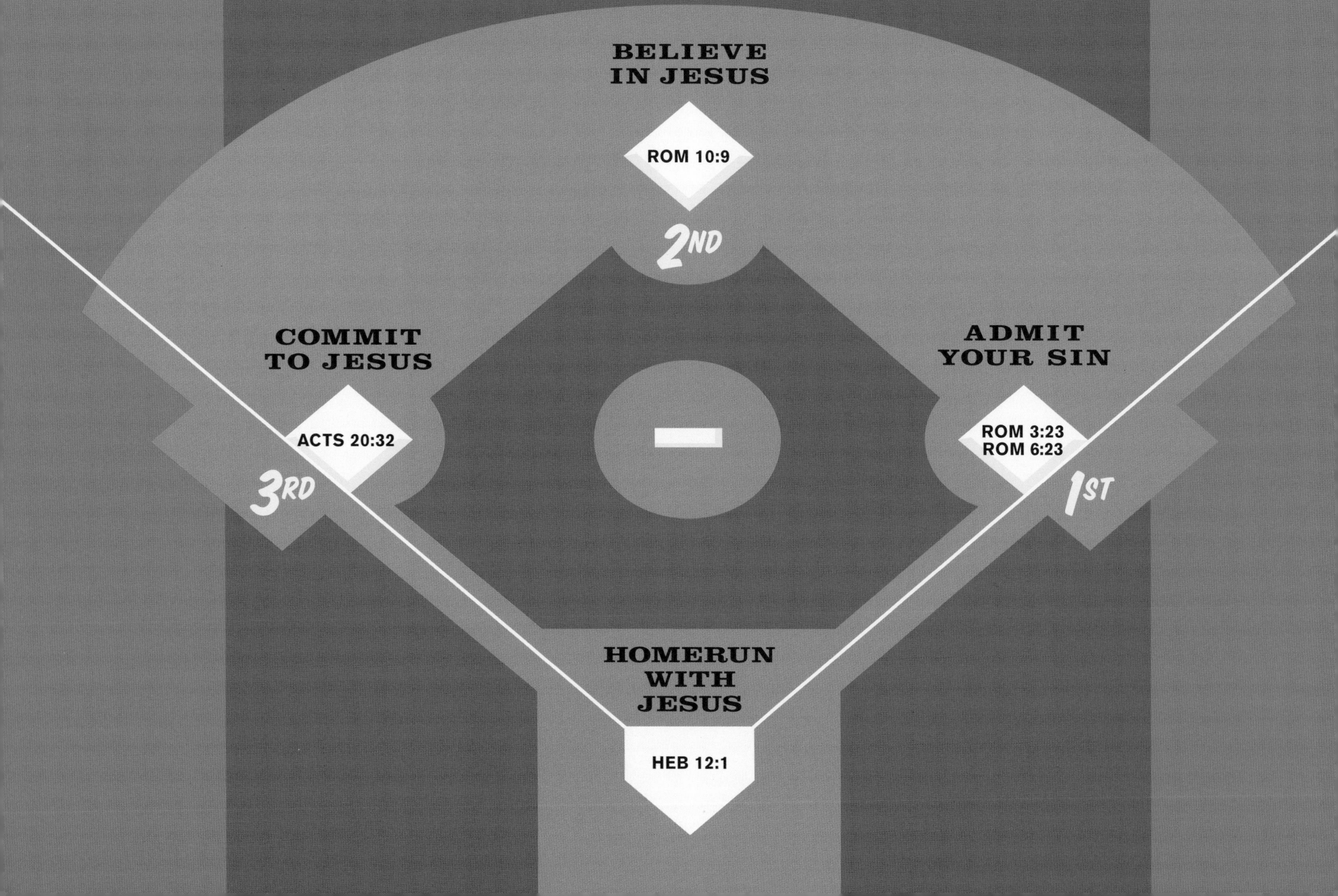

CHECKLIST

- ☐ COLOSSIANS 3:17
- ☐ EPHESIANS 6:14-17
- ☐ 2nd TIMOTHY 4:2
- ☐ 2nd TIMOTHY 3:16-17
- ☐ 1st PETER 2:13
- ☐ 1st TIMOTHY 4:12
- ☐ 1st CORINTHIANS 12:18

- ☐ LUKE 6:48
- ☐ 2nd TIMOTHY 2:15
- ☐ PSALM 121:1-2
- ☐ PSALM 35:9
- ☐ PROVERBS 17:17
- ☐ 1st THESSOLONIANS 5:11
- ☐ 1st PETER 3:15

- ☐ PSALM 23:4
- ☐ JAMES 4:6
- ☐ PHILLIPIANS 3:14
- ☐ HEBREWS 4:12
- ☐ 2nd TIMOTHY 4:7
- ☐ PROVERBS 10:1

Chris & Kimberly Maiocco

Chris and Kimberly Maiocco have been married since June, 1991. They met in graduate school in 1990. Chris accepted Christ at age 22 at a Billy Graham crusade. Kim accepted Christ at age 7. They serve together in lay leadership at the First Baptist Church in Woodstock, Georgia. The Maioccos homeschool their four children: Christian, age 10; Jon, age 8; Michael, age 7; and Chelsea, age 5. At the age of 8, Chris's parents divorced. As a result, there were many men that helped shape his life through sports. He believes strongly in using sports to teach children. He has shared his love of athletics with Kim, their children, and the many lives he has touched through coaching. Chris and Kim believe their greatest call is to share their love of Jesus with their children and to pass this heritage on through their generations while discipling other families to do the same. The Maioccos make their home in Roswell, Georgia.

"God-loyal people living honest lives, make it easier for their children!" - Proverbs 20:7 THE MESSAGE

Tom Cox

Tom began his relationship with Jesus Christ when he was a young child. He seeks to share God's saving love and grace through the gifts of art and creativity that God has blessed him with. In his opinion, there is no creative limit to a person walking in the freedom of The Creator's brush stroke. He lives in Woodstock, Georgia, with Connie, his wife of 10 years, and their two children, Ty, 7 years, and Taryn, 2 years. They have been active members of the First Baptist Church of Woodstock for the past 9 years.

Tom has been a designer for 12 years and has drawn all his life. You can see his online portfolio at www.tomcoxdesign.com. He has an Associate's Degree of Fine Arts from Reinhardt College, and a Bachelor's Degree in Journalism from the University of Georgia. His biggest influence for loving the game of baseball was his dad.

"We have not received the spirit of the world but the Spirit who is from God, that we may understand what God has freely given us." - 1 Corinthians 2:12